Vacate Victimville

Anthologies for Hurt, Hope and Healing

Written by Vernice Cooper

ISBN-13: 978-0-578-86828-8

Publisher's Note

Acknowledgments

To God, who has kept me whole in broken places.

To my husband, Raymond Cooper, who trusts God enough to love me for better or for worse. Thank you for your prayers and guidance on this journey.

For my son, Ryan Cooper, God's first gift to us. Stay humble and fiercely innovative. You inspire me to take more risks and trust the process.

For my daughter, Riley Cooper, God's promise. Thanks for sitting with me many hours working on your own short stories while I wrote this book. What a gift to write a book with and for someone you love. Together we will break generational curses that have plagued our family for decades.

A special thanks to the many coaches, mentors, friends and family that have encouraged me over the years. Your lessons and love are invaluable.

To all aspiring authors. Keep writing. Someone is waiting for your story.

Table of Contents

Introduction

I *set fire to the page.*

Amused by the blaze and intrigued by the black smoke that filled the air before compromising my lungs, I let my anger burn to a crisp. The heat it produced comforted me. So, I did it again, only this time to bask in the warmth of its therapeutic value. I wasn't in love with the fire, I was attracted to the light it gave in dark places. The freedom it gave me. The way it grew me closer to God and further away from my chaotic childhood was transformational. So, I continued as a serial arsonist, secretly setting fires between pen and paper as I wrote expressions of hurt and hope. Now, I stand on the ashes of the lyrics, poems and stories I never told. Boldly resigning as Mayor of Victimville, I offer you this final tour.

In this book, I hope you can explore the fire that burns within. This anthology is for people who may be navigating anger, forgiveness, betrayal, or any other bumpy road in life. Victimville is a place in the human mind where painful experiences, thoughts and feelings get caught in a cognitive traffic jam, where reasoning is stalled, and judgement is impaired.

May you reflect on the experiences of the characters in this book to help give insight into your own struggle. In these ten fictional short stories, I invite you to employ your curiosity, investigate the mystery of human suffering and discover your path to healing.

Journey

Go with me,

Take my hand,

Your steps must be precise.

Along the way,

You may encounter

Tragedy and strife.

Keep my hand,

Don't let go.

The stops are very brief.

If you let go,

You may get stuck

Longer than you need.

Every place in this small town

Seems big

when you arrive.

But you're equipped

with everything

Needed to survive.

Disappointment Drive

People often travel to Victimville by way of disappointment. When others fall short of our expectations, we tend to implode, causing harm to ourselves and people we love.

I took my last hit. I was sure this time. Bubba was like a son to me. Not the average teen junkie. He had a big heart. Good parents. Bright future. He used to always peep through the six-foot wooden fence as a child when we were getting high in the backyard. Until one day, he grew old enough .to hop the fence and join us. He laid there, stretched out on Sir Charles' lounge chair staring into my soul. Even the dope I was on couldn't protect me from the sorrow. I found myself standing at the gates of hell as the death recruiters called my name. So, I decided to do what any responsible addict would do, I reached over and closed the channel of communication. His eyelids, cold as freezer ice, left the skin on my fingertips numb.

I had a son his age that I neglected, so I could explore my crush with misery. I couldn't take any more hits — no more hits of the pipe or from the sweaty left palm of Sir Charles. I'm not even sure how I ended up here with Bubba, Sir Charles and everyone else in this dump. I knew better. These weren't the cards I was dealt. Somewhere along this journey I reshuffled the deck and picked this joker. Sir Charles knew he was selling Bubba too much dope for one pop. But who was I to judge? I began to scratch at the needle wounds along the median cubital vein - a vein known to addicts in my town as the voice of reason. I could literally feel my blood boiling and the obsession revisited.

Officer Raincom, the only female probation officer in the valley, interrupted my internal dialogue. "Are you ready, Ms. Fintley?" Officer Raincom asked.

Tears began to gather at the bottom of my eyelids. I suppose this was my first time authentically surrendering to the disease of addiction. I had never really considered residential treatment as an option for my recovery and quite frankly, I was hoping another stint in county jail would suffice. I beat heroin in jail before and the detox kicked my ass. The only problem was that heroin came and found me at the steps of the county jail upon release and always welcomed me back with open arms. People always spoke highly of Pasadena, California, the City of Roses. People were so busy admiring the beauty and aroma of the roses that they didn't see the thorns on the bush. Pasadena was economically and socially complicated. The palm trees that shaded the sidewalks were a distraction to gang activity, drug wars and sex trafficking. A life I knew all too well.

The social worker from the Department of Children and Family Services assured me that I would have a good chance of getting my son back if I completed this residential rehabilitation program. I only had five months left of reunification services. Five months to get clean, secure housing and obtain a job, according to Judge Riser. The thought of never seeing him again began to overwhelm me. It was bad enough that I had not seen Joshua and Tristan in years. Winston was my youngest, now thirteen. I still had time to get better.

Officer Raincom grabbed my bag and held my hand as we walked towards the bus. I kept looking back to see if Sir Charles would come to see me off. He said he was going to the liquor store to get a pack of cigarettes and never returned. I was worried that he might have had car trouble and asked Officer Raincom if I could use my cell phone one last time to check on him. She denied my request. She wasn't the worst probation officer I had ever had, but I knew she didn't like Sir Charles. Perhaps that's why she was sending me out of state for treatment. Probation and Social Services must have put their resources together this time around. It was uncommon for the two government agencies to collaborate, especially on my behalf.

Officer Raincom helped load my belongings under the bus and wished me good luck. I wanted to hug her but there was no space between my pride and shame.

"Alright then, Raincom," I said sarcastically.

"Well, is that all you have to say, Malice Renee Fintley?"

We both burst into laughter. I always knew I was in trouble when she called me by my full government name.

"It's Mrs. Malice Renee Fintley to you, Officer Raincom," I replied.

I frequently reminded Raincom that she was old enough to be my daughter.

"Thanks," I whispered, but Raincom was already walking back towards the station. Perhaps I could have said it louder, but I think she knew I was grateful for another chance. Besides, she said she would contact me at the rehabilitation facility.

I boarded the bus, scanned for the first available window seat and sat down. The partially reclining seats were comfortable beyond imagination. Everyone had their individual television secured in the headrest of the seat in front of them. I reached for my phone to call Sir Charles and tell him how nice this bus was. I forgot Raincom took my cell phone, so I was left with nothing but my own pity, the lasting effects of this morning's dope, and overwhelming anxiety.

The rain tapped against the window at a steady pace. Its rhythmic pattern complimented the sound of the bus engine in the same way the bass guitar compliments the piano in a jazz ensemble. I suppose I fell into a brief trance when my eyes tracked a single raindrop down the windowpane. It paused momentarily; long enough for me to notice both its transparent and reflective qualities.

I remembered walking along Castaic Lake with Momma when I was young. She would always ask me to look in the water, while staring at my reflection and ask, *"What do you see?"*

I always told Momma what she wanted to hear. In fact, I had it rehearsed. "I see a pretty girl with a bright future," I pronounced with great confidence. I knew it would make Momma's day to hear me say those words. After spending time at the lake, I would rush home to look for the same image, but my bath water didn't possess the same reflective power of the lake.

"Everything and everyone has its unique purpose," Momma would say. However, my young mind always challenged the status quo. Why couldn't I swim in the bathtub or bathe in the lake? Why couldn't both bodies of water offer the same reflective power? I challenged most of what Momma told me as a young girl. It wasn't because I was disrespectful or raised with poor manners. It was simply because I wanted more for her. She was smart, beautiful and educated. However, she lacked the ability to leave Daddy, and watching her suffer until the day he died was painful for both my brother James and I.

"Are you awake?" asked a dark-haired woman as she leaned over her chair and into my personal space. Preoccupied with my reflective process, I failed to acknowledge or even make eye contact with this space invader. I pretended to yawn to discourage her from further inquiry.

"There are blankets in the bin above your head," she explained.

"Thanks," I replied as I shifted my focus back to the window.

"And my name is Perla," she added.

At this point, I was so annoyed that I only offered her a thumbs up to affirm that I heard her name. Perla turned back around in her seat. I felt relieved. I never had many female friends. It's probably Momma's fault. She told us that Daddy left her for Aunt Karla, and I've been skeptical of women ever since that time.

Karla wasn't my mom's sister, but she was like family because she and Momma went to grade school together. I thought losing Daddy to another woman was the worst thing that could ever happen to a child, until he returned home. I'm still mad at Momma for letting him come back home. For taking care of him when he grew ill. For making sure he was buried properly with military honors for his time in the US Army. He was a decorated general with many awards to prove it, but I was never impressed. How can a man honor his country with his whole heart but betray his wife and kids?

Daddy returned home on my prom night. He said he wanted to see me off on my biggest day. He ruined that moment for me. I still remember Momma cooking what seemed to be a feast for a party of ten. James and I thought she was trying to impress my prom date and his parents before they picked me up. The scent of her special occasion White Diamonds perfume, the infectious smile on her face and the pride she displayed when Daddy finally returned home sickened me. She acted as if she had cheated on Daddy and needed to plead for his forgiveness. I was so angry. My prom date, Samuel, never spoke to me after prom and he is not to blame. I didn't talk that night. I didn't eat and I never stepped foot on the dance floor. Preoccupied with the make-up session happening at home, I had zero capacity for fun. In fact, I took my first hit of dope that night. Not sure if it was to numb my disappointment in Momma or punish Daddy, but there I was, shuffling the deck.

Poker's Jokers

A Queen can stand with great authority,

Until a pair of Jokers

Pulls rank,

And robs her of her crown.

Lost in the reshuffle,

She's now paired

With a kingdom-less king

In an unfamiliar town.

Bluff

I can't see your hand
partially covering your face,
hiding the tip of your nose,
concealing your pearly white teeth,
silencing your razor-sharp tongue.

I can't see your hand
shooting up the dope,
Tying up that rope,
Rolling up the joint,
Pouring liquid sin.

I can't see your hand
Because
You
Don't
Have one.

Anger Alley

Anger Alley is a very narrow, cave -like pathway that runs adjacent to Disappointment Drive. It's covered with a darkness that even the sun's rays can't illuminate.

He opened the untampered safe and retrieved his semi-automatic AR-15. Hands trembling, he searched feverishly for his ammunition. Stan always told people he fought in two wars, Operation Desert Shield and The Black American War. He knew that fighting for his country abroad wouldn't exempt him from the ongoing race war at home, and he was sure that his unwelcoming neighborhood might have known who ransacked his home, painting racial profanities on the kitchen walls.

"Stan?" his wife called out. But the revenge fantasies were overwhelming his consciousness. "The police are here; they want to talk to us!" she yelled down into the basement.

Stan could hear the officer's radio transmitting police chatter and it snapped him out of his daze.

"I'll be right up," he replied. Jet lagged and compassion fatigued, the Franklin family were glad to finally return to the United States. Their ten-day trip to the South Caribbean gave them all a new appreciation for the privileges and luxuries in the

United States. It was only a partial vacation for the family because Stanley was a humanitarian at heart. He wanted to expose his children to sandy beaches and the impoverished communities of color that are exploited at their expense. This year, Stan got his children involved by having them choose books they've enjoyed reading over the years. They taped five American dollars to the back of each book as a hidden reward for children who actually read the books to completion. Stan would always figure out a way to give back to a world that he believed gave him so much.

Weeks before the trip, His children found great joy taping money to over 100 books. Although they complained about the heavy luggage, they reaped the rewards of philanthropy. During a day trip in Antigua, they rode through a rural part of the country on an ATV tour handing out books to the children who lined the streets. Many of the children waved at the caravan of ATVs which drew the attention of Stan's daughter, Lisa. Nicknamed P.I. for her detective skills, she was the family researcher and detective. She had so many questions about the lack of adult supervision and the barefoot children who stood on the curbs of the streets. Consumed with social politics, Lisa took lots of notes that were sure to be a part of her next blog.

As they pulled up to their home, Stan Franklin noticed one of the gates leading to the backyard was left ajar. In an effort not to alarm his wife and kids, Stan didn't express his panic. As a trained military specialist, he knew in his gut that something was wrong. He recalled how he meticulously locked down his home and the perimeter before their departure and knew that his efforts were compromised.

"Stay in the car!" Stan asked of his family. Nick didn't hear his father's commands. The music blaring from his ear pods was loud enough to cause permanent hearing loss.

"What are we waiting for?" Nick yelled with curiosity.

Moments later, Stan returned to the car.

"Call the police!" yelled Stan towards the car.

"For what?" his wife asked as she slowly stepped out of the vehicle.

"No, stay there," he demanded. "We've been robbed."

Lisa's eyes grew to the size of two large tennis balls. She clinched her hands together in prayer because the thought of the police frightened her. Lisa was the first ten-year-old in her class to start a YouTube channel to expose police brutality in her community. Her first video on badge bending exposed local cops who took honor in killing Black men.

"No, Mom," Lisa bargained.

"They won't ask about Daddy's military service or charitable contributions when they get here!" she cried to her mother.

Regina dialed emergency services, despite her daughter's plea. They sat silently in the car, waiting for the police to arrive.

Once the police arrived, Regina explained that her husband was inside of the home assessing the loss. "Yeah, don't go in there, I'm filming you," young Lisa said with her cell phone recorder pointing towards the officers.

Regina emerged from the stairs with her husband.

Stan spoke to officers in an inaudible voice, leaving only hand gestures and facial expressions for Lisa to interpret before police followed her father into the home.

"Mum, can I at least get out of the car?" Lisa asked of her mother who was standing outside the home pacing in front of the car.

"Yes, honey, but you will need to stay out here with Nick; police might want to collect fingerprints," her mother explained.

"But that's exactly why I need to be in there, Mum," she spoke with her English accent. Nick always teased his little sister for going into character when she was getting into investigative mode.

After thirty minutes, Lisa joined her mother in a brisk pace alongside the front lawn. Lisa bombarded her mother with questions and begged her to go inside and check on their father. Although her mother never responded verbally, she did offer Lisa looks that only a mother raised on collard greens and black-eyed peas could give. Regina wasn't a woman of many words. But the looks she gave could offer everything from celebratory praise to negative sentiments. Certain looks she gave even Lisa knew not to challenge.

Nick lowered his headphones and finally exited the car because his cell phone battery was about to die.

"Can we go in now?" he asked. Regina gave him the *no* look, so he stood.

"Front door open," the family alarm sang.

"Finally!" Lisa said as she followed her mother and brother towards the front door.

The first officer carrying a large briefcase led the charge. Behind him was a second officer escorting Stan in handcuffs and carrying an assault rifle.

Lisa tried desperately to access the video on her expired phone battery.

"What happened, Stan?" Regina asked.

"Call our lawyer," he responded, avoiding eye contact with his family.

911

In the event of an emergency,

Please dial 9-1-1,

Unless 9-1-1

Is the 1

You can't count on.

Because you can't

Breathe,

Sleep,

Jog,

Play,

Without being the victim

And

The perpetrator.

Betrayal Blvd

Many people travel on Betrayal Boulevard to avoid traffic and get to their destinations quicker.

S he asked me to pack up Stephan's belongings after he went home for the day. Three, flat, cardboard boxes were neatly stacked on her desk as she gave the orders. I was still too new and too desperate for her approval to inquire what this meant for my office mate. But I did what was requested of me.

I will never forget his face that day. He was so frank. He smiled and said goodbye to everyone like he usually did each evening. We tapped elbows, and I tried not to make eye contact. *Why would she be having me pack up his belongings?*

He had been an intern with the firm for almost a year. He was graduating next month with honors from Harvard Law. So, I packed up his stuff that night, and he, nor his belongings, returned the next day. Jane announced that Stephan no longer worked for the firm during the morning reports meeting Friday. She later thanked me privately for packing up his stuff but never spoke of it again.

Jane was a great employee. She arrived to work early, took on extra assignments, and was the last to leave each day. She wore an infectious smile and was well respected by her peers. At home, Jane would spend countless hours boring her husband with work related proposals for cases she was hoping to be assigned. In fact, she told me her family said she lived for her job. It was a huge part of her identity. I only came to know her devotion to her work when I started as her intern six months ago. Late night text messages and early morning calls were expected of me from the day I started.

Named Alejandra Lupe Jane Espinoza at birth, only one other person at work, besides me, knew her as anything other than Jane Ramirez. Her long blonde hair and piercing blue eyes afforded her unwarranted privileges in the workplace. I found out very early that she did not want to be associated with her heritage when she scolded me for decorating her office space for Dia De los Muertos. I let my White privilege get the best of me that day by assuming she would enjoy my Pinterest inspired decor.

Her colleague, and close friend Nancy, often reminded Jane of their cultural roots by speaking to her in Spanish.

"Buenos Días, Lupita?" Nancy would ask each morning of Jane during team check in.

"Well," Jane would typically answer in English. Her subtle resistance to everything reminiscent of her Mexican culture detectable. But Nancy was relentless in her quest to challenge Jane's assimilation.

I frequently referred to my phone's Spanish translator to keep up with the under-breath mumblings of my boss.

Nancy and Jane appeared to be close friends from my observation. They allowed me to tag along on their hump day lunch meetings each Wednesday. The laughter they shared was contagious. I often found myself laughing at the jokes about Ron's wrinkled shirts, mismatched socks, or crooked ties.

He was the brunt of so many jokes during those lunches and in the office.

He was a sweet guy, mildly tempered and soft spoken. Ron was tall with a medium build, long chiseled chin, and jet-black hair. He wore a man bag and was adorably clumsy - an easy target in an office full of alpha males and fiercely educated females. But the incident I saw last week in the parking garage had me contemplating my loyalties.

Who was I to disrupt the workplace camaraderie and friendship between my direct supervisor and her friend? How could I possibly tell Jane that Nancy kissed Ron just before he dropped to one knee? That her best workplace buddy was kissing the guy they frequently teased during lunch breaks. Besides, Nancy never wore the ring he presented to her that night. I thought to myself, *maybe Nancy dropped something onto the ground that night and Ron was just retrieving it. Perhaps the kiss meant nothing.*

I was so fearful of being seen that evening that I stayed sunken into my driver's seat long after they both pulled off in their respective vehicles. I didn't sleep much that night. Too much was at stake. I couldn't jeopardize this excellent work opportunity, study for the BAR exam and keep my sanity. My silence was my saving grace and my biggest regret. I came to learn; it wasn't the only shady thing happening at the Firm.

Weeks passed and I began to question my investigative skills. *How could I possibly be an aspiring attorney if I only had circumstantial evidence about this workplace affair?* In the office, Nancy and Ron rarely made eye contact, let alone spoke to each other. Nancy continued making jokes about him during our Wednesday lunches and they laughed hysterically. I giggled at some of the jokes so that my demeanor wouldn't be alarming.

When the Equity Partner position opened at the firm, everyone expected that Jane would get the job with little to no opposition. Jane had a great working relationship with the Equity Partners and had expressed interest in promotional opportunities. She often offered me advice on advancing in the workplace and securing a permanent position after the internship. Jane participated in leadership conferences and took extra online courses to prepare herself for the new role. When the job initially became open for interested applicants, Nancy urged Jane to apply. Nancy convinced her that she was the best candidate for the job. I was reasonably confident that Jane would promote to Equity Partner, which would benefit the minor details of my resume tremendously.

Nancy was in the know; she started as a law clerk like Stephen and worked her way up in the firm. She had no desire to make Partner and never appeared to pose a threat to Jane's promotional aspirations. However, something I learned during those Hump day lunches with Jane and Nancy, was that there had never been a minority or female Equity Partner in the firm. The Partners were all male, within the same age bracket and all attended Ivy league schools. I was so inspired by the possibilities for the shift in organizational culture at the firm, but I did not make my excitement known.

The much-anticipated day had come. The blind interviews, secret whispers and anxiety were finally coming to an end. I didn't know who exactly applied and competed for the position, but I knew Jane's promotion would mean opportunities galore for my career. I sat in the boardroom, looking over the city from the seventeenth-floor trembling with excitement. I stashed a bouquet of red roses and a heartfelt card that took me days to write under my desk. But even my prestigious education at Columbia University couldn't prepare me for what happened next.

The room filled quickly with all twenty-seven attorneys silently occupying available seats along the boardroom table. Matthew Arbuckle, Equity Partner and COO commanded the attention of the room with his presence.

"Without further ado, I would like to announce our newest equity partner," Arbuckle said. He explained the rigorous interview process and the need to continue to grow and evolve the firm by diversifying its culture. He stated that the new partner has been diligent, consistent, and fierce. I could feel my eyes tearing up for this monumental moment.

"And the new Equity Partner for Prestige Law Firm is Ronald Temple," he announced.

My heart dropped to the souls of my feet. My jaw followed. I glanced over awaiting Jane's rebuttal, her complaint, her storm. I looked at Nancy who was gleaming from ear to ear and noticed she didn't seem to share the same level of shock and surprise. She knew, I thought to myself. Nancy knew that her secret boyfriend would get the job despite her constant praises of Jane and pushing her to apply. Jane stood first, applauding the decision. Her peers followed suit. But I couldn't stand. My heart still buried in my shoes, I had to consciously defy the laws of gravity just to get to my feet. My hands made contact but there was no sound.

"There is one more announcement I would like to share," Matt explained.

"Ron's brother, Ryan Temple will be joining us as the new Law Clerk, replacing the position Stephan Cooper previously occupied," he explained. Nancy, still smiling, made eye contact with Jane and shrugged her shoulders as if the news were new and foreign to her. There was no further business, and everyone filed out of the board room. I waited for Jane. I knew she didn't care much for human contact but everything inside me wanted to offer her a hug.

"Close the door behind you," she demanded as she paced her office floor.

"Hijo de puta!" she yelled.

I knew now wouldn't be a good time to pull out my phone and access my Spanish translation app, so I stood quietly near the door.

"Poor Stephan. I fired him because Nancy said he was making advances towards her," she said looking at me as though she wanted to strike the vase that stood between us.

Even then, I couldn't bring myself to tell her about the love affair between Ron and Nancy.

"Jennifer Metzker, did you know?" she asked.

I took two steps back towards the door as she physically drew closer to me. I didn't speak. I didn't answer. I just looked towards the floor. I wasn't sure if she was talking about the workplace romance between Ron and Nancy, the promotion, or why Stephan was fired so I did what any aspiring attorney would do. I plead the Fifth.

Art of Betrayal

The absence of truth is a lie
Untold,
So that deception with
good intentions
Can be deemed
Acceptable.

Yet.
the currency of loyalty
Is so cheap.
That it's value
Only reflects one's
Worth.

Integrity compromised for
The gain of ego,
That will be exploited
When met with the
Same inevitable
Betrayal.

Resentment Road

Resentment Road runs parallel with the major freeways and will carry you through town. However, because of the multitude of potholes and uneven pavement, the drive time is almost doubled from one end of town to the next.

Five months passed without us speaking a single word. One year since I've last seen him. The ungrateful little bastard could have at least called me on my sixtieth birthday. Shannon tried to defend him by showing me that he "liked" the pictures she posted on social media at my party. She always defended his actions. A son can do no wrong in their mother's eyes. But when it came to Junior, we were not on the same page. I was a good father. We were good parents to a grown son that was keeping something very precious away from us, our first grandchild.

Our conflict may have started during his last season of little league baseball. He wanted to quit in the middle of the season. As his coach and father, I couldn't let him do that. He needed to learn what it's like to keep his word and honor his commitments. When I explained to the then nine-year-old son of mine that part of being a good man and a good person starts with finishing the season, something changed between us. He heard me but he wasn't convinced. I remember that look in his eyes that showed me his sorrow and his disappointment. I still get that look from him when he comes home. A look as if he feels sorry for me. He wanted to learn to play the piano instead of baseball. He apparently loved music, but I was too blind to see it until he majored in Music in college.

I helped my father build Elliot Construction from the ground up. I did everything he asked of me from my birth to his death. I even became the Foreman he wanted me to be. I was an obedient and loyal son. Junior never had that level of respect and admiration for me like I had for my father.

Shannon began prepping me in September for their arrival. "Be nice, Charles," and "Mind your manners, Dear," were her constant reminders. And I planned to do just that. Why Junior would choose Halloween weekend, my least favorite Holiday, irritated me. He also knew his mother hated Halloween but of course she went out and bought every Fall decoration and Halloween accent she could find. I helped her decorate, draping spider webs across our vaulted ceilings to impress an infant, a woman I've never met, and a grossly disrespectful son didn't exactly put me in a festive mood. I mostly engaged out of my love and admiration for the most beautiful person I knew, my better half.

"I'm so proud of you, Honey," she said as I hung skeletons from the ceiling. I smiled. Flattered that after all these years, I could impress her with the little things.

"But I need you to dig deeper, Chuck," she explained. I stared down from the ladder at her to make eye contact. I knew what she was asking may very well be more than I could deliver.

"And what instructions have you given your son?" I asked.

"Don't change the subject Charles Elliot! You and I both know this is bigger than a small quarrel between a young boy and his father. I'm impacted by all of this, too, ya know," she said as she stormed off to the bedroom. While I was skilled in manual labor and repairs, the emotional repair she required of me at times didn't come with specific instruction or tools.

"I'm sorry, Babe, but don't you think your son has been unreasonable?"

"Unreasonable, Chuck?" she asked, lifting her head from the pillow.

"Yes, Shannon, he didn't even tell us he was having a baby."

"He told me, Chuck. He asked me not to tell you, Honey. He didn't want another one of his personal choices to be judged by you," she explained. I stared at her. Betrayed. Triangulated. Unappreciated. She had a different relationship with Junior. She was his confidant, protector and friend. This left me with no role to fill in his life. I lost my job as his hero and Dad long ago. And I could tell I was losing her, too.

"Dig deeper?" I asked.

Asking questions for clarification were as reliable as my channel locks.

"What is it that really bothers you about Junior?" she replied with a question. I offered her years of specific examples where he was disrespectful. But she wasn't impressed. She didn't budge. She laid there like a three-week-old concrete foundation, waiting for me to build the frame.

"I don't know, Shannon. Your son just hates me for some reason."

"He doesn't hate you, Chuck, he misses you."

"Well, he sure as hell has a funny way of showing it."

"So do you!" she replied standing to her feet and pulling a wool coat over her shoulders. I offered to help her, but she declined. I knew it was hard for her to continue refereeing this match between Junior and I.

"Fix it, Chuck!" she hammered, submitting her resignation. Something about her demand felt like an ultimatum.

As the jet-black SUV pulled into the driveway, I watched Shannon scurry throughout the house checking everything from the dimmed lights to the refrigerator that she stocked three days ago. Her level of excitement was a heavy weight to carry. I did not want to be the person to take that away from her. I strapped on a tool belt, mostly out of nervousness and wanting a way out in case things felt awkward.

"Honey, they're here!" Her voice echoed throughout the home.

We opened the door and there stood my very own father staring back at me. Junior now twenty pounds heavier stood there in the very spitting image of my dad. I never saw the resemblance before their arrival. In his arms, a beautiful little boy that softened my heart at first sight, and a beautiful woman with long, black hair and deep, brown eyes.

Shannon lit up.

Grabbing for the child that poured out of Junior's arms and into the arms of his grandmother without fuss.

"Dad, this is Charles Elliot, the Third," Junior said.

"We call him Chuckie," the woman explained with a smile.

I turned around to remove the tool belt I had thrown on in a panic and placed it on the floor. I knew there was no tool that could help me fix this. The son that hated me had the audacity to name his son after *me*, after *us*.

I wrapped my arms around him and held him with a closeness my father and I never shared. It must have been a rather long hug because by the time our arms unlocked, we were all in tears.

Traffic Problems

The problem is
The accident ahead,
And the collisions
Of my past.

The problem is
The things others have done
Are in the rear view
Mirrored glass.

The problem is
I can't signal
Because my blinker
Gets ticked.

The problem is
The congestion you caused
Has made me
Very sick.

Vacate Victimville

Contentment Court

This prestigious residential neighborhood is perceivably peaceful and appealing to the natural eye. However, the comforts of Contentment Court come with a high price.

S he unlocked the front door and eased it open slowly with the tip of her shoe. With her toddler slumped across her left shoulder in deep sleep, she quietly carried the groceries and child into the home. She peeked around the door to get a glance of his recliner. There he was, sleeping with a can of Bud Light nestled between his hip and the corner of the recliner. She had mastered the science of not disrupting his afternoon nap and prioritizing his comfort. After carefully placing the groceries on the kitchen countertop, Nicole headed upstairs to lay her child in his bed.

At the entrance of his door, she paused long enough to notice the small troop of green toy army men lined up as if they were guarding the perimeter of her son's bed. Their defensive posture was alarming. He recently asked for more green toy army men and Nicole was beginning to understand the magnitude of her fears. She gently laid Nate onto his bed and meticulously separated his long golden strands of hair from her shoulder. She stood over his bed, admiring his innocence and hoping that the only trait he inherited from his father were his royal blue eyes.

As Nicole stood at the top of the stairwell, she tried to ignore the holes in the wall that were created in last night's fight, but her body remembered. Her heart began racing and her palms grew sweaty. The makeup covered bruises on her face couldn't mask her angst. She checked her Apple Watch to monitor her heart rate, which was now at 135 beats-per-minute.

She headed to her bedroom instead. She knew to place the grocery receipt on his nightstand to account for today's expenses. He didn't leave a grocery allowance today, so her only recourse was to use the credit card he heavily monitored. On the other nightstand lived her *happy pills,* so she indulged. The five-milligram prescription Ativan had become her closest confidant. Access to this non-judgmental friend was not an issue. Her doctor never questioned her early refills or inquired about her now two-year-old postpartum depression diagnosis.

Nicole took a deep sigh and headed back downstairs to get emotionally grounded. She proceeded to the living room and stood behind the reclining chair as he slept. She stared at his defenseless body, stretching her phone charger to its full length and considered a tragic revenge. She reached over the chair and slightly kissed his forehead. For this was home.

Fall represented many things, but for the Moore family, it wasn't the pumpkin spiced lattes or orange leave lined streets that were important. It was the beginning of the football season. Rick, a huge fan of America's favorite football team, the Dallas Cowboys, was already experiencing another disappointing year. Bad games resulted in tough days and nights. Nicole cheered for the Cowboys with all of her might because she understood how their losses would result in losses for her. But last night was different; the Cowboys won. Celebrations were warranted but never arrived. In fact, Rick was upset that Nicole was excited about the victory.

Removing groceries from the reusable bags, Nicole contemplated on what she would tell her mother. Last night after Rick fell asleep, she texted her mother an image of a rose. This was their code. The rose represented the promise. The promise that when Nicole was ready, she and Nate would leave Rick for good. But now she was stuck with a dilemma. There was no way to retract the rose. She tried desperately to delete the text last night, but her mother had already replied.

"See you soon," her mother's text read.

The anger outbursts are few and far between, she bargained with the bananas as she made space for them in the fruit bowl. Maybe it was something she had done to provoke his anger, she pondered while juggling an apple between her hands. She turned towards her dining room table to admire the centerpiece of flowers he bought her four days ago and smiled. She recalled the tears in his eyes, the tremble in his voice and the regret in his note he wrote after the fight last week.

She daydreamed about the beginning of their relationship. About the flight where the gorgeous man in the tailor-made navy-blue suit flirted during the trip. Intrigued by his charm and mesmerized by his distinguished appearance, Nicole felt lucky to gain the attention of a high-profile business executive. What are the chances that a small-town girl from Enfield, North Carolina, would gain the attention of such a prestigious man?

Twelve years her senior, Rick had never been married. His colleagues said he was married to his career before meeting Nicole and expressed their admiration for her, making Rick a better person. Rick's mother offered similar sentiments towards Nicole's influence on Rick prior to her untimely death last year. Their relationship started with fireworks. A Paris themed wedding on the sandy beaches of St. Marteen was more than she ever dreamed of. But the sweet and kind gentleman that swept her off her feet five years ago no longer existed.

Nicole heard a knock at the door. She rushed to the foyer of her home to answer the door so that it wouldn't interfere with Rick's nap.

"Mom?" she whispered with confusion while looking over her mother's shoulders.

"Yes, Nikki, it's me," her mother explained with a smile.

Nicole pointed towards the living room to signal where Rick was. Nicole stepped on to the porch to look around outside.

"Did you come alone?" Nicole asked.

"Certainly dear, I would never alert your father to problems in your home," her mother explained as she entered the home wheeling in a small suitcase.

"Mom, you can't just show up unannounced!" Nicole explained.

"Would you have preferred me to send the police, Nikki?" her mother muttered as she handed her daughter her coat.

Janet Flosden was the epitome of a snob. She had only been to visit her daughter's home once before when Nate was born, and Rick was working out of town. She toured the first floor admiring everything from the elaborate profiles of the crown molding to the glass cabinetry in the kitchen. Rubbing her fingers along the gray veins of the white quartz countertops, she nodded quietly in agreement with the remodeling choices Nicole discussed with her over the phone.

Janet stood in front of the television, staring at Rick sleeping and loudly cleared her throat to wake him. Nicole covered her face with both hands and feared the interaction between them.

"Janet?" Rick asked as he rose from his chair and stumbled over to embrace her with a hug.

Janet wrapped her arms around Rick and held him closely while smiling over his shoulder at her daughter. Nicole quickly adjusted her posture and asked them both if they were hungry.

"Yes!" they replied in unison.

Nicole made her way to the kitchen to prepare food while Rick and her mother talked and laughed in the family room. She knew in that moment that her mother had not come to rescue her and Nate. In fact, the peace she sought in her mother, on her cell phone and in her happy pills wasn't looking to be found. It was waiting to be created.

Next Flight

The skies aren't always friendly.

Some flights

Turbulent,

But mostly

Predictable.

When the cabin pressure increases

And my breath escapes me,

I look up for the oxygen mask

you dangle over my head.

It lands

On my face,

Relieved

Until

next flight.

Missing Cub

Tame the beast within

That roars at her

But not at men.

Find your inner cub,

The hostage plan,

Then set him free.

For while he's still held captive,

So are you

And so is she.

Grief Gateway

The biggest feature of Grief Gateway is Preservation Park, the largest recreational park in town. Here you will find the laughter of young children, the smiles of elderly onlookers, and the promises of greener pastures.

"**A**re you hungry, Madea?" I yelled down the hall after throwing my backpack on the kitchen countertop.

The aromas of cinnamon, nutmeg and melted butter piqued my curiosity. Madea typically made her sweet potato pies at least two days before Thanksgiving and I was eager to find out if at least one of them had been compromised so that I could sneak a slice. Besides, I was her favorite grandchild, and this was my favorite time of year. The first grandchild is always the uncontested favorite. My siblings and younger cousins were mere afterthoughts. Framed grade school pictures of me covered the living room walls. This was a point of contention for all of Madea's grandchildren. That's why I always came to visit early in the morning, so I didn't have to compete for her attention.

"Madea?" I asked again, as I searched high and low for her prized pies.

Madea liked to watch her recorded episodes of The Young and the Restless and General Hospital first thing in the morning. Her lack of response was surely an indicator that she was fully engulfed in some high-level adultery or exaggerated betrayal from her soap operas. We always teased Madea about the shallow storylines, amateur acting skills and constant drama in the soap operas.

I stood in the corner of the kitchen negotiating about which appliance I needed to unplug so I could start the thirty-year-old coffee pot Madea wouldn't let me replace. The large, red, Folgers coffee can glared at my resistance from the partially opened cabinet. My efforts to transition Madea to the likes of Starbucks, Peets Coffee or Keurig coffee pods fell short every time. I could never even finish telling her how coffee has progressed before she would clear her throat and start the song again.

"The best part of waking up, is Folgers in your cup," she would sing in her baritone singing voice.

While I vaguely remembered the commercial, the song would surely haunt me for a lifetime. It was her justification that no other coffee could compare to her beloved Folgers. Although I didn't particularly care for the taste of coffee, the smell of the coffee beans was comforting and familiar.

I could hear the cheesy dialogue blaring from her television as I carried the bitter, black coffee down to Madea's room. Shadow, Madea's standard poodle, was cuddled under her arms and glanced at me briefly to acknowledge my presence. It wasn't until then that I realized Shadow never greeted me at the door with her shallow bark.

"Madea?" I asked in a whispering voice of disbelief. I placed the coffee on her dresser and sat at the foot of her bed. Tears began to fall because the absence of her smile and lack of Shadow's bark were confirmation. I knew in that moment we lost her. Doctors tried to put her in hospice during the summer, but Madea's faith extended our time with her.

Pleading for her attention, I stood tall, singing the Folgers song with my hands covering my mouth.

"Madea, I can't believe you are sleeping through this episode," I explained as I carefully increased the volume on the TV. I returned to the foot of the bed. I rubbed her leg as if I was to wake her. It was cold to touch, so I placed a blanket over her and stared.

For some reason, I couldn't fully process what transpired. I continued to shift my eyes between the "box," as Madea used to call the TV, and her lifeless body.

Her house phone rang loudly, scaring Shadow and interrupting my internal dialog.

"Hello?" I answered with curiosity.

"Where's Nana?" my sister Charlotte asked. She referred to Madea as "Nana" just as the rest of the younger grandchildren.

"Hurry up, Kenya, I have to tell her about Bingo last night, so she knows who won the Blackout game," Charlotte asked of me with excitement and conviction.

"She's gone, Charlotte," I said with very little emotion in my voice.

"Where did she go this early in the morning? We already finished all the shopping for Thanksgiving," Charlotte asked with great concern.

"To heaven I suppose," I whimpered.

"Heaven? Heaven!" Charlotte began screaming and crying so loudly that Shadow offered me her condolences with her large puppy dog eyes. Charlotte had questions I could not answer. And her loud cries were sure to disrupt Madea's transition, so I hung up.

I retrieved my cell phone from the kitchen to call Momma. Facial recognition didn't recognize this ugly cry, so I had to punch in my passcode to dial.

"Momma?" I asked with curiosity.

"Yes, Kenya. I'm at work, what is it?" she replied in a scurried voice.

"Madea, Madea, is, ummm, she's ga... ga... gone Momma!" I tried to explain without turning into the same blubbering mess as Charlotte.

Momma never replied. She didn't even say goodbye or ask any questions. I was unsure if I had made myself clear or if Momma knew what I was referring to, but shortly after she hung up, Madea's house phone started ringing off the hook. I knew in that moment that Charlotte had likely called my aunt Lena, the family messenger.

I returned to Madea's room and gently kissed her on the forehead, my tears dripping onto her face. I grabbed the Blue Magic hair grease and a fine-tooth comb, so I could begin separating her long curls that gathered at the top of her crown for one last time. I knew Madea would never forgive me if I let everyone's last memory of her be with wigless bed hair. She took pride in her appearance and taught me a lot about being a well-kept woman. Attempting to postpone my own grief, I gently braided her hair and fought back tears as I pondered.

I didn't know Madea's God. The God that made a way out of no way. The one that got Uncle Chris out of jail, Sharene from next door off drugs and paid for Granddaddy's 1978 Ford F150 when he was laid off. I plopped down onto the floor beside Madea's bed, raking my fingers through the aqua blue shag carpet she adored. It had a permanent dent caused by my sister and cousins that would sit there while Madea greased our scalps and gossiped on the house phone.

The memories came flooding back. As a child, I sat secure between her legs as she unapologetically combed my hair harshly before Sunday School. I think she combed and brushed with such force because I never admitted that Granddaddy and I would stop at the local bookie and place horse racing bets when he picked me from Momma's each week. She would ask me every week. But as much as it pained me to lie to Madea, I was more afraid of snitching on Granddaddy. That was my buddy. He snuck us candy and all kinds of treats. I loved Madea, but I couldn't give up my candy pusher. I kept his gambling secrets, even after his death.

I sat there sobbing, remembering how she used to send me cards in the mail. She was good with words. Poetic at times, inspirational mostly. I picked up her Bible sitting next to me to see if I could find some comfort in her God. Our God.

There were so many folded pages, tabs and bookmarks, I didn't know where to begin. The worn down, black, leather cover was transitioning to gray. I was trying to pull myself together before Momma and the calvary arrived, but I needed answers. I was surprised to find my name and birth date etched in the front cover, along with the same information for every grandchild. I chuckled. Madea always sent birthday cards and we all thought she had our birthdays memorized. Not knowing where to start, I just opened the bible in half and found Psalm 119. My eyes were drawn to verse 169, so I read it aloud so Madea could hear me. But the King James Version didn't resonate.

"Madea?" I asked with tears in my eyes and laughter in my voice.

"I'm going to read this from the New Living Translation, is that okay with *thee?*" I laughed to myself. We always joked about the King James Version of the Bible.

I grabbed my phone and read aloud.

O Lord, listen to my cry.

Give me the discerning mind you promised.

Listen to my prayer.

    Rescue me as you promised

Let my lips burst forth with praise,

    For you have taught me your principles.

Let my tongue sing about your word,

    For all your commands are right.

Stand ready to help me

    For I have chosen to follow your commandments.

O Lord, I have longed for your salvation,

    And your law is my delight.

Let me live so I can praise you,

    And may your laws sustain me.

I have wandered away like a lost sheep.

    Come and find me,

For I have not forgotten your commands

I closed the Bible app and sat my phone down with new insight. I looked up at Shadow still resting in Madea's arms and smiled. I foolishly thought I was helping with Madea's transition but realized she was helping me with mine.

Down to the Pew

Seven rows down on the right-hand side,

Far from the babies that rarely cried,

I rest on your lap and closed my eyes.

I knew it was coming just after the tithe.

Do you want to go down to the Pew?

The ushers swayed and marched and stepped,

The Pew is where you could leave your regret.

The choir acknowledged His grace in each hymn.

And back to me you would look again.

So, you took me down to the Pew!

I folded my hands and bowed my head

And when you weren't looking, I peeked ahead.

I saw you crying,

And I grew scared,

Why do people go down to the Pew?

I learned the Lord's Prayer

So, I could keep along,

A few good scriptures and even some songs.

I sat up straight so you could now see,

I was ready to go to the Pew!

Laid down my burdens,

Forgave some folks,

Cried just like you,

But rose with hope.

I learned so much at the Pew!

I'm grateful you allowed me to tag along,

And thanks for your prayers that kept me strong,

Rest now, Madea,

Your work here is through.

I will see you again at the Pew!

Codependency Cul-de-sac

Some consider this a dead-end street but it's not. Its U-shaped curve at the end of the cul-de-sac is designed to allow drivers space to change directions.

S he always peaked out of the plantation shutters when he pulled up to the house. Spying to see if his equilibrium was intact. He could, if sober, park in the narrow space she left in the driveway without allowing his tires to touch her beloved artificial grass.

Last night, I saw her outside with a flashlight going through his car. So, I prepped the tea kettle promptly at eight a.m. for our morning session. She stormed across the street, with her evidence bag in hand, and pounded on my door.

"Tea?" I asked while opening the door.

She walked right by me, tears in her eyes and frustration covering her face.

At the table she unloaded her bag of clues. A receipt. An empty bottle of Jack Daniels. A hotel key card. A Planner. And Mouthwash.

"Does he think I'm stupid?" she asked of me.

I knew better than to answer any questions she had about her husband's affairs. Once I told her that it wasn't a serious problem, and she didn't speak to me for weeks. I poured the boiling hot water into her cup.

"Black or green?" I asked.

"Thank you," she replied.

I stared at her with confusion.

"Thank you for giving me a choice, Kimberly," she cried.

"Let's go with green," I decided for her.

"It's known to help with blood pressure and matters of the heart."

We sat and sipped in silence. This was our process. Lucky for Michelle, I was retired and had plenty of time for her rants. I purchased flowers from the farmer's market yesterday because I know weekends are hardest for her. Weekends she would reach her high and hit her low.

"So, what do we have here?" I asked as I shuffled through the clues she spilled on the table.

She grabbed the receipt first. Before handing it to me, she ripped it in half. I wasn't sure if it was my job as her neighbor and friend put the pieces together or just hold it so she wouldn't have to.

"He was there last night," she replied.

We sipped again. Harry wasn't a bad guy. He was a very sweet man. After my husband passed away, he took on the responsibility of mowing my lawn and always bought my newspaper up to my doorstep on his way to work. He was also a great father. He raised two respectable young boys. Sometimes I figured that Michelle was preoccupied with Harry's affairs because the twins were now grown and off to college.

Instead of asking what was on the receipt, a conversation I knew she wasn't ready for, I chose a different path.

"How did you get this?"

"I went through his wallet while he was sleeping," she responded with conviction.

"Well, maybe I should have made you a cup of black tea since it doesn't sound like you got much sleep," I explained.

"Not a wink."

When things were really bad, Michelle would stay up all night looking for information to confirm things she already knew. She found pleasure in proving that he was a liar. But she was also complicit in his behavior. Last week she came over and asked me to call his employer and pretend to be a nurse at the hospital. She wanted me to help her excuse his absence because there was no way she was going to let him go to work. In fact, she left both sets of his car keys that morning at my house. He thought he had lost them, but she was trying to prevent him from getting another early morning ticket for driving under the influence. She even asked the clerks at the supermarket not to sell him alcohol last summer. "You must sleep, Dear," I warned her.

"How can I sleep while he is frolicking in the streets in the wee hours of the morning?" she asked.

"Do you see this?" she asked, while lifting the empty bottle of Jack Daniels.

I nodded in agreement. She went on to explain how Harry had no more chances with her. A claim

I've heard a million times. A proclamation that carried no weight. She once bought a suitcase here with her and asked if she could stay for a few days. I declined her request with love. She was not my responsibility and I needed to draw a line. Besides, how can I uphold my title as the nosey neighbor if I'm taking in strays? I had a reputation to defend. I was an observer and information gatherer. A therapist and a trusted friend. I could not pick sides on this very narrow street. Especially against a man that reminded me so much of my late husband, Robert.

"And this!" Michelle asks as she lifts the Marriott key card and stands to her feet.

She paced the kitchen floor, staring down on the yellow and white tile flooring I so desperately wanted to replace. Placing one foot in each square she began hopping around like a child.

Now sitting back in my chair, I sipped my tea until she ended her show.

"Are you done?" I asked, after letting her hop for five consecutive minutes.

"No, I'm not done. Just tired," she said as she returned to a seated position on her chair. Those words had meaning beyond her physical exertion of energy. It was also representative of her mental state. She was tired but never done. She loved him. She loved what they built. She loved their image on the local billboards advertising their joint real estate company.

"More tea?" I offered.

She lifted her cup. I reminded her of the story when Robert and I were going through a rough patch in our marriage. I told her of all the foolish things I did to try to control his behaviors. I admitted the poor choices I made so that she may be able to see her own contributions to the chaos in her home. However, she needed to close this deal. She always wanted resolution, even when there wasn't one available. She was the toughest client in my imaginary private practice. Even Mark down the street who admitted to me that he was a thief, a professional kleptomaniac, would be easier to persuade than Michelle.

"What about all of this?" she asked, pointing to her latest pile of evidence.

"Perhaps you have found exactly what you've been looking for," I replied, pouring her second cup of tea.

"Are you saying that I'm asking for it?" she inquired.

"What I'm saying, Dear, is that sometimes we look for things we know to be true. We are looking for confirmation to validate our behavior," I lectured.

"So, are you saying I need to divorce him or what?" She stood back to her feet.

I glanced at the chair she vacated, sipped my tea and waited to see if she was going to transfer all of her anger and outrage back across the street. We sipped in silence. I knew that she needed rest. I know how insomnia can impact a person's emotional state. I read about it on Google. This is where I found my second career as the neighborhood trusted counsel. It amazed me how much psychologists were paid to listen to people's problems, challenge them intermittently and allow them to come to their own conclusions.

"Sometimes, I wish it was another woman he visited in those hotel rooms," she whispered, breaking the silence.

"How would things be different?" I asked from my repertoire of cool, therapeutic interventions I learned online.

"Another woman would be easier to accept because I can't compete with alcohol!" she cried.

I watched the anxiety subside as she melted back into the chair. The exhaustion from trying to control his behavior overwhelmed her. No matter how much she deprived him of food, sex and attention, he was sure to find a way to spend time with the love of his life: alcohol. Michelle didn't understand the peace that alcohol offered her husband. It isn't argumentative or judgmental. It is reliable and accessible.

"Should I tell him the cancer returned?" she asked.

"Are you trying to guilt him into obedience?"'
I responded with a question while heating the kettle
for another cup of tea.

"You're right. I won't even tell him."

me

I don't see me

Even when

They tell me to look

In the mirror

To find

Myself,

My joy,

My peace.

All I see is

Your reflection

Looking back at me.

Forgiveness Freeway

The main freeway in town offers exits every two to five miles, giving residents and visitors many opportunities to choose a place to begin the healing process.

There I was again. Standing alone on the edge of the cliff with my arms spread wide like an eagle ready to soar. I could hear my breath echoing along the canyon as I looked toward the sun, now towering over the hills and exposing the shaded valleys. I slid my right foot forward to the edge of the rocky mountain top, my toes seeking a break from the sun scorched ground. It was too hot to stay there on the cliff, so I leaned forward and plunged down.

I woke up gasping for air and reaching for my inhaler. I glanced over to see if he was still asleep, but he wasn't. He stared back at me with great concern. We were both met with the eerie silence that spilled over from yesterday and the day before. I wanted him to cuddle me and remind me that it was just a dream. But I didn't make my request known. I was still punishing him with silence. He was sure to engage in a verbal debate but never contested the silent treatment. My pride suffocated my vulnerability.

Attaching the spacer to pump, I inhaled the remaining albuterol and exhaled a sigh of relief.

I slipped my arms in the red, silk robe he bought last Christmas and stormed across the room to demand his attention away from whatever social media platform that had his undivided attention. Last night's argument was about money, the night before about chores. I wasn't even sure we knew how to have a decent conversation anymore. The only thing that filled the silence between us were intermittent periods of explosive dialogue. Mostly me nagging, as he called it.

After weeks of pretending to be asleep when he was on his phone in bed, I had finally got the access code. I needed to know if he had moved on because we were unfamiliar roommates at his point.

143143

It was our pager code when we met as teenagers back in 1997. Before cell phones were accessible to the average person, we were subjected to a single line display of numerals. It meant, I love you.

Why he would use our old school love language for his cell phone passcode was beyond me.

We went our separate ways after high school. Colleges in different states. But distance and time would be no match for the love we had for one another. We stayed connected over the years via text messages, calls and social media. During major holidays we would both visit our respective families that still lived in East Oakland. I always looked forward to our Thanksgiving tradition of walking along Lake Merritt to rid ourselves of the fat and toxins of holiday foods. Until three years ago, when that walk ended with the sweetest kiss and a proposal. I'm still not sure how we lost our way. I had convinced myself that our inability to conceive a child was building resentment in him, but I was too afraid to ask.

He left his phone on the nightstand charging while he went to take the trash bins out to the curb. I knew now was my time to take a quick peek at his call log and search history. What I found broke my hurting heart. Frequent calls to his mother and sister. Text messages of encouragement to him. The search history was hardest to deal with. I could see him outside chatting with the neighbor, Greg, so I further investigated. With several tabs still open on his phone, I read:

> *Dealing with a grieving wife*
>
> *How to restore your marriage*
>
> *How to save your marriage*
>
> *Loving someone angry*

The lump in my throat was persistent. I couldn't swallow the shame that gathered there. While I've been browsing the internet, posting about women's independence and queendom, he has been trying to figure out how to save what was left of this three-year marriage. The texts he sent to his mom reminding her that he still washed my car every Sunday and left me breakfast on most mornings was probably my biggest reality check. He was fighting for a marriage that I had already left. Tears fell, creating burgundy-colored spots on my red robe.

I looked out the window and saw him smiling and laughing with Greg, probably about sports. I wanted that, too. The joy. Back into our home. Still attracted to the 6'2" medium-built, caramel-complexioned man that towered over both Greg and the trash bins, a smile peaked under the tears.

"Can we talk?" I asked as he entered the door.

"What are you doing with my phone, I don't go through your phone!" he asked, grabbing the phone from my hand.

"What happened to us?" I asked. Curling into a fetal position in the chaise lounge. He sat close, occupying the space left on the seat.

"I don't know, Layla, but I miss you," he said, grabbing my left hand, interlocking our fingers. I wept like a grieving widow. He kissed my forehead and said the words I longed to hear.

"I love you," he said over and over. Attempting to make eye contact by lifting my chin with the tips of his fingers. I knew that he loved me. But I wasn't raised to be receptive to vulnerable love. The type of love that required more weakness than strength was foreign to me.

My mother never apologized to me or to anyone for that matter. I learned very young that being sorry was a sign of weakness. This was the world she knew and the lessons she saw fit to teach me for survival. She was a single mother, raising a daughter to be self-reliant and independent. She always encouraged me to be unapologetic. But in that moment, the unapologetic strength that I wore as a badge of honor was the very thing that was holding me back. Holding us back.

"I'm sorry," I said finally.

The words left a chalky taste in my mouth that dehydrated my dignity and starved my ego. Here, I could only feast on humility. I was sorry for not being able to bear children. Sorry for being mean and stonewalling him every chance I got. I was sorry for not being sorry. A warmth covered my body. Not because of his forgiving touch, but a familiar warmth from the sun on the cliff. I had jumped down many times. But today, I landed.

Off-ramp

Returning the

Luggage you left

In my heart,

For it's yours

To keep

And store.

I'm giving it back

To set myself

Free,

For I deserve

Much more.

Freedom comes at

A heavy price,

Many aren't willing

To pay.

But suffering is optional,

And I'm planning

To exit

Today.

Boundary Bypass

Many use this alternative route to avoid traffic, road construction delays and stop lights. Equipped only with few stop signs, travelers rarely slow down and are more likely to drive through the bright red signs.

L akeisha rushed to the front of the school and stood at the third redwood tree closest to the Kindergarten apparatus. It wasn't like her to be late to the campus, but she knew it took about three minutes for children to gather their belongings and get their last-minute hugs and shoves. She watched hundreds of children spill into their family cars and onto the campus sidewalks. Some of the young children that crowded her ankles stopped to say, "Bye Dayna's mom." She embraced the idea of losing her own identity and taking on the role of being a mother. The parking lot began to empty as she waited, waved and closed the car doors for other parents.

Mrs. Lakeisha Toffman volunteered at her daughter's school and sat on the PTA board as the fundraising liaison. Best known for her revenue generating cookie dough sales, she was as popular as school moms come. She checked the time, now fifteen minutes after the final bell, Lakeisha decided to walk towards her daughter's third grade classroom.

Dayna was a lively eight-year-old that loved to hang out with her peers.

Once Lakeisha arrived at room E102, her teacher, Mrs. Turnage was erasing the board.

"Good afternoon, Mrs. Turnage. Have you seen Dayna?" she asked.

"Hi, Mrs. Toffman. She was here in class today but left with everyone else at the sound of the bell," the teacher replied.

Lakeisha canvassed the campus, checking bathrooms and asking school campus supervisors and administrators about her daughter's whereabouts. She called her husband who was working out of town to ask if he had heard from their daughter. In the school office, the attendance clerk made a school wide announcement over the PA system.

"Dayna Toffman, please come to the school office, your mother is waiting for you."

Lakeisha stood at the entrance of the office door waiting for her eight-year-old daughter to run towards it, but she never showed.

Office staff made inquiries of her mother.

"Is there anyone else who may have picked her up?" they asked.

"No, I pick her up on Thursdays and Fridays," she replied.

"Well, her emergency card also lists a Margaret Jenkins. Have you contacted her?" the clerk asked. Lakeisha stormed out of the office to call her mother but to her surprise, her mother's voicemail came on. Her mother rarely had her phone off unless she was at the casino. With it being a Friday afternoon, she was sure her mother would likely be at Thunder Creek Casino with her friends. The panic returned.

"Call the police!" she begged the clerk.

The sun began to set and still no sign of Dayna as local police searched the school grounds. School cameras were placed throughout the campus, but there was no operational budget, so they were not actively recording. Night fell and Lakeisha, along with Mrs. Turnage and a beat officer, exchanged information for any updates.

Margaret called.

"Mom, Dayna is missing!" Lakeisha said, crying.

"She's not missing, you are so dramatic. I picked her up and took her to the movies," her mother explained.

"Margaret Anne, how could you do this? I'm here with the police. We've been searching for her for hours!"

"Get off your high horse, Lakeisha! No one has stolen your princess," she said before hanging up the phone.

Lakeisha notified the police still on campus and thanked the parent volunteers and staff that stayed and searched for her daughter. This wasn't the first time Margaret had crossed a boundary. Last summer, she straightened Dayna's hair without her permission. And over the Holiday break, she gave her granddaughter taffy candy, which resulted in an emergency trip to the orthodontist the next day.

Margaret didn't see her actions as reckless or inappropriate.

As her grandmother and the matriarch of the family, Margaret didn't feel the need to obtain permission to spoil her granddaughter. But, the blatant disregard for Lakeisha's desires had come to a head once and for all. This violation was egregious, and Lakeisha was finally ready to address it.

Lakeisha sat in the car in front of her home and prayed for courage to end her mother's reign over her life. Dayna met her mother at the door with a hug that felt like hours wrapped in a few seconds.

"We need to talk, Margaret," she said to her mother.

"Oh, what now, Dear? You are so sensitive."

"Sensitive?" she yelled.

"You practically kidnapped my daughter!" she explained.

"Kidnapped?" she laughed.

"Yes, you took her without my permission."

"No, Dear, you told me you didn't have plans today."

"Yes, but that doesn't mean pick up Dayna without my permission! I was worried to death," she explained.

"That's because you are a hypochondriac," she said as she walked away.

"Gimme my damn house key!" she demanded of her mother. Margaret turned around with a shocked look on her face. She had become the victim, a familiar tactic she used to avoid being the villain. Margaret removed the key from her key chain and threw it on the floor in front of her daughter's feet.

"You will need me before I need you," she warned Lakeisha.

The door slammed behind her.

Text messages from Margaret flooded Lakeisha's phone throughout the night. She chose to spend the night holding her daughter and being grateful for her safe return.

At sunrise, she read the text messages from her mother calling her horrible names and insulting everything from her marriage to her college education. Her mother repeatedly called her "bougie" and warned her that she was going to fail. Lakeisha found the messages hurtful and fired back. Reminding her mother of her awful parenting skills and poor life choices.

Her mother, now fully rested and sober, replied via text, "Well, I had a horrible childhood, too, but I don't complain." Lakeisha paused and reflected on the manipulative skills that her mother once again employed to be the victim. Instead of replying to her final text, she saddled up and got back on the high horse she fell down from.

Paper Cuts

I didn't draw this
Line
For you to cross.

I didn't pick this
pen
So, you could stab.

I didn't grab this
Paper
For you to fold.

I didn't pick you,
Mom
But the lessons are
Gold.

Hey. Dotty

A dotted line

May suggest

There is something

To connect

Or divide.

Bypass

Or separate.

Redefine

your boundaries,

so that people

Don't occupy

space

not intended for them.

Recovery Road

The least maintained road in Victimville is tough on tires because of the uneven asphalt but it will lead you to your destination.

The first few weeks were *hell*. He didn't just hate me, he hated himself and life as he knew it. Some days I wished he lost both of his legs because he wasn't half the man that he said he was. The wheelchair was the only thing that I still had compassion for. The weight it carried couldn't be measured in pounds. The energy that transmitted from his soul was piercing. His eyes, demonic.

He frequently blamed the drunk driver, but he, too, was drunk on the day of the accident. Everyone in town was talking about the collision. There was much debate about who was at fault in that Thursday evening wreck that rallied a community uproar and overdue conversation about drinking and driving.

There wasn't much to do on Thursday evenings in SLO besides eat, drink and attend the infamous Farmer's Market. It wasn't your average Farmer's Market lined with healthy vegetables and fruits; it was a whole vibe. San Luis Obispo couldn't have a better nickname than SLO because there was nothing fast paced about the area. Nestled along the central coast of California, SLO is home to a prestigious polytechnic university, a short drive from the ocean and neighbors with a state prison for men. But for us, it was home.

I chose to stay here after college because I enjoyed the slower pace. I made many friends in SLO and met the love of my life, Annissa. I introduced her to the family last Christmas, and she was appalled that my family called me Coal. She understood colorism on a deeper level than I ever cared to know. She wanted me to denounce the name Coal, once my mother told her she nicknamed me that because of my dark-complexioned skin. Annissa found Coal, short for charcoal, demeaning and disrespectful. It wasn't until I started this job, my dream career, that I would come to understand the impact that my dark skin, my race and my Black experience may have on the patients I worked with. Every day I complained about Donald's presence. Not out loud to my colleagues, but to myself in the car on the way there. He was the epitome of a racist White man.

I dreaded coming into work on Mondays and Wednesdays. He would arrive before my shift. Impatiently waiting in the lobby and asking all types of unnecessary questions to our medical assistants. Even though he didn't believe that physical therapy was helping him or restoring his strength, he never missed a session. He told everyone that he was trying to prove a point to his insurance company that he needed a monetary settlement and not a physical therapy program. We did our best to accommodate his needs and tolerate his poor behavior.

My colleagues made formal complaints about his use of foul offensive language in the clinic during his first two weeks of treatment. I avoided making reports against patients because I knew policies established to protect employees from the harassment of patients were vague. Plus, I enjoyed the challenge of working with his physical limitations. He was only the second amputee I've worked with and I loved new opportunities that challenged me professionally.

Something changed after the discovery of his evil enabler. While positioning Donald for upper thigh strengthening, a small half quart sized bag of pills fell onto the floor. I reached to pick them up and return them to his possession.

"It's not what you think, Boy," he explained.

"James. My name is James," I corrected him. Calling a grown Black man *boy* was the closest you could get to calling him a nigger in this part of town without consequences. So, I was sure to correct him. Every. Single. Time. Everyone always gave me kudos for dealing with Donald when in fact, I was just tolerating him. Calling me *boy* was far more offensive than the family nickname Coal.

He snatched the pills from my hand.

"It's none of your damn business!" Donald yelled.

"I don't want to know," I shrugged, returning to the strengthening exercises.

"I need these. Your people don't understand what it's like to be a hard worker and not able to work," he said.

"My people?" I asked.

"Not many Black people like to work, you are just different, Boy."

"James, not Boy, and I am not different," I stated without further explanation. This was the most dialogue we had in months, so I indulged.

"You are getting stronger physically but mentally you've got a long way to go, Man," I said with a chuckle.

Donald looked down towards his legs, face hidden from me as though he had never heard a compliment before. All he could see was what had been taken from him. He didn't understand the value of what was left. Without accusing him of anything, I told him about my sister and her addiction to pain pills and other drugs over the years. Without interruption, he pretty much let me tell him my entire life story as we moved from exercise to exercise. I may have gained some humanity points when he learned my father was in the military, but I think it was my sister's story that intrigued him most.

"Where is she now?" he asked, as if interested.

"Headed to rehab, last time I heard," I responded. He offered me the space to talk, so I explained that part of healing physically is being able to mentally believe that you are capable. I flooded his ears with hope while the gates were open and receptive.

That day was hard for both of us. Angry tears poured down his face when I asked if his wife would like to join one of our future sessions. I assumed by the diamond-encrusted gold ring on his finger that he was a married man, hated even by his own wife. He initially didn't answer the question, but the tears spoke for themselves. I knew that being married to this bitter young man was probably too difficult for any woman to endure.

"Her Gods punished her for marrying me," he finally spoke.

Instead of asking for clarification, I let silence fill the empty spaces in dialogue. It was hard for me to watch a man cry, even one that I despised. So, I continued with his strengthening exercises, looking in the opposite direction.

"We were celebrating Diwali when she grew ill," he said. He went on to explain how much he and his late wife looked forward to Diwali, the Festival of Lights.

"She wore the most beautiful red and gold Saree," he cried.

"Saree?" I asked.

"She was the most beautiful person I've ever met. Her physical beauty was just a glimpse of the inner beauty she possessed," he said, while searching for tissue.

He went on to tell me how they met in college and were married shortly thereafter.

During our session break, I hung out in the staff break room and Googled Diwali. It was then that I realized that his wife was of Indian descent, the

Saree, a dress worn during Diwali. I was perplexed on what good the woman he described saw in the man I met three months ago.

"You doing okay, Man?" I inquired.

"Yeah, I just can't believe she's gone."

"Gone?" I asked, while assisting him back into his wheelchair.

He looked up at me and nodded his head up and down. A flood of emotions came over me. *Do I let him sit in his sorrow or hug the evil dude and offer him my compassion?* I chose the latter. He held tight.

"I'm sorry, Man. I didn't know," I said, releasing him from the hug and sitting in the chair next to him.

"No one really knows how hard it is," he said.

"You will get through this, all of this," I offered.

"All I have left of her is Mallika," he said, pulling out a picture of a young, brown-skinned toddler with long, dark hair and big brown eyes.

"Is this—"

"My daughter," he interrupted.

"Well, now there's going to be trouble!" I warned.

"Trouble?" he asked.

"Good trouble," I winked.

Ten minutes of lecturing took place. Now in the driver's seat, I explained to him how the rehabilitative skills he is learning are transferable to real life. How he needed strength to recover physically and emotionally. For Mallika.

"Thanks, Man," he said.

"So, I'm a man now?" I laughed.

"Do you prefer Boy?" the evil still lurking. Maybe my deep brown skin reminded him of the night of the accident. The rejection of his wife's family who were dark like me or even the dark future he dreaded.

"The name is James, or you can call me Coal," I replied.

get To The
garden Side

If you're stuck in the forest perhaps by choice,

Or even just by chance,

Look to the sky for moisture and rain,

And don't forget to dance.

When the music stops, and the rain has dried,

Go to the garden instead.

For in the garden, the dreamer lives,

With hopes for seasons ahead.

Plant your seeds here on the garden side,

Where life flourishes from the sun's glow.

For in the forest, Where The Wild Things Are

The darkness will stunt your seeds' growth.

No one will hear your forest cry,

You will only become its prey.

Hide in the shadows...camouflage,

And seek the garden by day.

The garden is planted intentionally,

You must nurture and remove the weeds,

For in this place, you control the fate

Of every planted seed.

Teach others to dwell on the garden side,

For this may be their time

To plant, to grow, to dream again,

And finally, to shine.

About the Author

Vernice Cooper is a dynamic motivational speaker, poet, author, and a Licensed Marriage and Family Therapist who is determined to use her education and experience to inspire, motivate and transform lives. Her life experience of overcoming family addiction and trauma, paired with her professional experience fuels her passion to guide people, particularly women, out of a "Victimville" mentality. Using real-world examples, humor, and short storytelling, Vernice sheds light on how resilience transforms the way we live, love, and heal. Vernice currently works as a clinician specializing in Addiction Medicine and Recovery Services at Kaiser Permanente, owns her own consulting business, Joy Road Solutions, and is the author of her debut book, Vacate Victimville.

Connect with Vernice www.vacatevictimville.net

Made in the USA
Las Vegas, NV
29 April 2022

48161217R00080